We are a community dedicated to advancing the artisan baking profession with a priority on education. This book is a reflection of that mission. We are proud to be part of this pioneering effort to educate young consumers and young bakers about the benefits of making bread with whole grains and minimal ingredients. It's never too soon for children to learn about making good food choices!
—*The Bread Bakers Guild of America*

Text copyright © 2018 by Kim Binczewski and Bethany Econopouly
Illustrations copyright © 2018 by Hayelin Choi

READERS to EATERS
12437 SE 26th Place, Bellevue, WA 98005
ReadersToEaters.com

Published in cooperation with the Bread Lab at Washington State University, Mount Vernon
Sponsored by the Bread Bakers Guild of America

Distributed by Publishers Group West

Whole Wheat Sourdough Bread Recipe courtesy of Jeff Yankellow
and the Bread Lab at Washington State University, Mount Vernon

Photos courtesy of Philip Lee, Kim Binczewski, and Washington State University

Printed in the USA by Worzalla, Stevens Point, WI (6/18)

Book design by Red Herring Design
Book production by The Kids at Our House
Special thanks to our co-editor, Karin Snelson

The artwork in this book was created digitally in Adobe Photoshop.
The text is set in Caecilia.

10 9 8 7 6 5 4 3 2 1
First Edition

Cataloging-in-Publication Data is on file at the Library of Congress
ISBN: 978-09984366-0-9

To my daughter,
Josephine Iris—
my favorite baking partner
and inspiration for each
and every day. —K.B.

For my hardworking
mom, who raised us on
store-bought, plastic-wrapped
bread. You taught me more
than any university. —B.E.

For my mom, who
constantly supports
me to cultivate my
imagination and
curiosity like Iris.
—H.C.

It was a sleepy Saturday morning for some people, but Iris had to wake up early. All of her pets were hungry! And animals never sleep in on weekends.

Iris needed to hurry if she was going to feed her dog Charlie, two cats, three rabbits, four fish and five chickens before Aunt Mary arrived. Iris liked to call Aunt Mary "Plant Mary" because she was a plant scientist. It made Aunt Mary laugh every time.

Charlie barked. Aunt Mary was here!

She was all hugs and smiles and boxes and bags, and she was on a mission. "Let's turn your kitchen into a bread lab, Iris!" she said. "I hope you're up for making some whole wheat sourdough bread... from scratch! How's that sound?"

"Woo-hoo!" Iris loved bread. Toast with butter and blackberry jam especially.

She was definitely going to need her notebook today.

Aunt Mary pulled a jar from her bag slowly,
like it was a treasure. "Iris, meet Flora!" she said.

Iris peered deeply into the jar, but saw only goo.

"She's my starter," Aunt Mary explained. "To make bread
you need a *starter* to start the process."

"Why did you give your starter a name?" asked Iris.

"Because I think of her as a pet!" said Aunt Mary.
"Flora is full of microbes—creatures so small
you can see them only with a microscope.
I feed her every day, just like you feed
Charlie here."

"I want to feed Flora!" said Iris. "What does she eat?"

"Flour and water," said Aunt Mary.
"Sounds delicious, right, Charlie?"

Charlie would happily eat flour and water.

"When the microbes in Flora eat, they release bubbles," said Aunt Mary. "Those bubbles make bread rise. And the bubbles are why bread is so **hole-y!**"

"Wait a minute… What?" said Iris.

"*Hole*-y as in bread with lots of little holes!" said Aunt Mary.

Iris didn't miss a beat.

"*Hole* wheat bread!"

"Exactly," said
Aunt Mary.

Iris picked up the jar of goo. "So, can we feed Flora now?"

"Actually, I just brought Flora in that jar to show you what a starter looks like," said Aunt Mary. "I used Flora to create a sourdough mix. Yesterday I put a tablespoon of Flora in this bowl, along with some whole wheat flour and warm water, and stirred it all together.
Now look! It's puffy and still growing! Smell it... It's yeasty, sweet—and just a bit tangy to put the *sour* in sourdough."

Iris sniffed the sourdough mix. "It smells like grass and... lemons!"

Iris poked the pillowy mix with her finger. It sprang right back up. "I think I'm hungrier than a microbe. I could cook eggs and toast for breakfast! Would you like some, Plant Mary?"

Charlie wagged his tail so wildly that Aunt Mary laughed. "Absolutely! Looks like we're all hungry. Good timing, too. The sourdough mix still needs more time to rise."

As Iris munched her toast, she picked up the package of bread and started to read the ingredient list. But it was full of words she couldn't pronounce.

"Wow, did you bring all this stuff to make *our* sourdough bread?"

"No need! Our recipe has only four ingredients," said Aunt Mary.

"Just four?" asked Iris. "Okay, let's see... The sourdough mix has Flora, whole wheat flour and water, right? What's the fourth thing?"

Aunt Mary waggled the salt shaker.

"Salt!" said Iris.

"Right!" said Aunt Mary. "We have everything we need to get started."

"It's feeding time," Iris whispered into the bowl. She measured
exactly the right amount of flour, water and salt—and then
added each ingredient to the sourdough mix. Iris imagined
the tiny microbes in Flora happily gobbling up the food...
and burping up bubbles.

"Use your hands to mix it all together," said Aunt Mary.

Iris washed her hands, then dug in. The sticky dough
felt good, oozing between her fingers like mud pies.

Aunt Mary leaned over the bowl. "Great work, Iris.
Now it needs to rest. But not us—let's clean up our bread lab!"

"Are you ready for the next step? Kneading the dough!"
Aunt Mary put the gooey glob on the kitchen counter.

"*Needing* the dough?" Iris asked.

"Ha!" said Aunt Mary. "Yes, we *need* it.
But we also **k-n-e-a-d** it.
Kneading makes the dough stronger and less sticky."

Iris stretched-folded-scraped-and-turned the oozy dough
again and again until her arms felt like they might fall off.
"Is the dough strong enough now, Plant Mary?"

Her aunt gave it a poke. "I wish I could say yes, but the dough
still needs you."

"Then I'll knead it!" said Iris. She flexed her arm muscles
like a superhero, and kept on going.

After the kneading was finished and the dough had time to rest,
Aunt Mary showed Iris the next step... folding.

"Stre-e-etch, fold, fold, fold... fold," Iris chanted.

"Now we let it rest again," said Aunt Mary.
"Then we do this two more times."

Iris made sketches of every step
in her notebook.

Iris could see the bubbles form while the dough was resting. "The microbes are busy—it's like magic," she said.

"Magic? More like science!" said Aunt Mary.

"Our bread is aliiiiiiiilive!"

"Can the dough pleeeease be ready, Plant Mary?" begged Iris.

Charlie whimpered.

Aunt Mary laughed. "You're both in luck. It's time to shape the dough." She showed Iris how to fold the dough into a log to fit the loaf pan.

"The dough needs about three hours to rest, so now we can take a break, too," said Aunt Mary.

"*Finally*," said Iris. "That means we have plenty of time for a picnic in the park!"

"What a feast!" said Aunt Mary. "And all the food you brought—apples, peanut butter, blackberry jam, chocolate and crackers—came from plants! Did I ever tell you why I became a plant scientist?"

"I don't think so," said Iris. "Why did you?"

"Ever since I was your age, I wanted to grow food. Now I help farmers grow food," Aunt Mary said, feeding a crumb to a hungry ant. "In fact, the flour for the bread we're making came from wheat grown by farmers I know."

"I never knew plant science had anything to do with food," said Iris.

No one thought about plants more than Plant Mary did. Iris loved that about her.

Time flew by as they ate their lunch, identified dandelion parts and found animal shapes in the clouds.

When Iris and Aunt Mary got back home,
Iris screamed. "NOOOOOOOOOOOOOO

All she could see was the
pan of dough... and Charlie's drooling jaws!
All that kneading, for nothing!

Iris lunged for the pan just in time.
The bread was saved.

"I guess Charlie wanted to be our bread tester," said Iris.

"Good thing he didn't eat that dough, because it's still rising," said Aunt Mary. "He would be one sick dog!"

Iris imagined Charlie swelling up like a hot-air balloon and floating away.

"Let's get this dough into the oven," said Aunt Mary.

Iris thought the smell of baking bread was the best smell in the world.

Finally, Aunt Mary opened the oven door.
"It's ready!" She took the loaf pan out to cool.

CRACKLE!

Iris could hear the crust crackle and pop.
"It even *sounds* delicious," she said.

POP!

POP!

CRACKLE!

Charlie barked. Iris's parents were back.

"Mom! Dad! We turned the kitchen into a bread lab!" said Iris.
She held up the loaf like a trophy. "Who wants to try our special
home-baked whole wheat sourdough bread?"

Everyone did, of course. Especially Charlie.

"Mmmmmmmm

Aunt Mary, Iris and her parents all gathered close.

Iris took a big bite of her slice. "Mmmmm…" she said, smiling at Aunt Mary. They really did it! They baked their very own loaf of bread. And everyone loved it.

Charlie liked his crunchy bit of crust, too, but he was easy to impress.

mmm…"

Iris opened her notebook and wrote:
Our bread tastes nutty, sweet and a little bit tart.

Aunt Mary leaned over to see her notes.
"Hey, that's a pretty good description of you, Iris," she said.

"And you, too!" said Iris.

Our bread tastes nutty, sweet and a little bit tart.

FUTURE SOURDOUGH PROJECTS

Muffins
Scones
Pretzels
Pizza
Waffles

Iris couldn't wait to bake with Aunt Mary again.
It was a good day in the bread lab.

Charlie thought so, too.

BREAD FACTS
A BAKER'S DOZEN*

MICROBES

1 People all over the world love to eat bread, whether it's pita, challah, bagels, pretzels, roti, naan, crumpets, flatbread, focaccia, tortillas or pizza.

2 Bread making always starts with two ingredients: flour and water.

3 Flour is made of grain, and grains are seeds. The process of grinding grain to make flour is called **milling**.

4 Wheat is the most common type of flour, but other grains—including barley, rye, oats and buckwheat—are also used to make flour.

5 Whole wheat flour contains all three parts of the wheat seed—bran, endosperm and germ—full of vitamins, minerals and fiber that make whole wheat bread particularly nutritious and delicious.

6 The secret to making sourdough bread is tiny microbes of bacteria and yeast—including lactic acid bacteria such as *Lactobacillus* and wild yeasts such as *Saccharomyces* and *Candida*.

*A **baker's dozen** is the usual dozen—12—but with one extra!

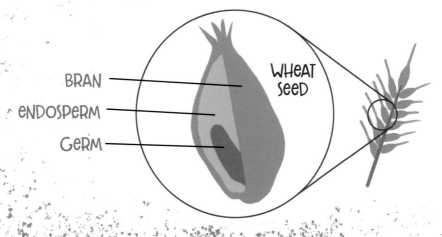

BRAN

ENDOSPERM

GERM

WHEAT SEED

7 Wild yeast and bacteria float around in the air and live on seeds and in flour. When you add water to flour, these microbes feed on the sugars in the flour and multiply. So, with just flour and water, you can create a bubbly mix of microbes. This mix is called a **starter** because it starts the bread-making process. You can keep your starter alive for years.

8 When microbes eat, they release bubbles of carbon dioxide (CO_2). These bubbles make bread dough rise and create the holes you see in slices of bread. These microbes also produce acids when they eat. Lactic and acetic acids give sourdough bread its famous, wonderfully sour taste and smell. Amino acids add the sweet, nutty and toasty flavors.

9 The process of yeast and bacteria eating sugars in the dough—and then producing gases, acids and alcohols—is called **fermentation**.

10 When it's time to start making your bread dough, you add starter, flour and water to create what we call a **sourdough mix**. Other names for a sourdough mix include preferment, leaven or levain, refresh, poolish and biga.

11 After you've added flour, water and salt to your sourdough mix, you're ready to start working your dough into whatever shape you choose, whether it's a loaf or a pretzel.

12 Experienced bakers find that sourdough bread tastes better after it has had time to cool, which allows the flavors from the flour and fermentation to develop. But hot bread, fresh from the oven, is hard to resist.

13 April 1 is National Sourdough Bread Day in the United States.

APRIL
1

WHOLE WHEAT SOURDOUGH BREAD

GET READY TO BAKE

The first step in baking (and also in conducting scientific experiments) is getting your tools and ingredients together. Then, it helps to create a rough timeline for your recipe. This careful planning helps you prepare—both physically and mentally—for what's ahead! Sourdough bread takes about 24 hours to make, from start to finish. But most of those hours are resting time for the dough—and for you—while the microbes do their work to make bubbles and build flavor.

WHAT YOU NEED

large bowl
measuring cups
measuring spoons
dough scraper
dish towels or plastic wrap
8" x 4" loaf pan
nonstick spray or oil

INGREDIENTS

starter
whole wheat flour
water
salt

TIMELINE FOR BAKING

Sourdough Mix: 12–15 hours, mostly resting time
Bread Dough: 8–10 hours for mixing, kneading, folding, shaping, resting and baking

SOURDOUGH MIX

1 cup whole wheat flour
½ cup water, warm to the touch
1 Tbsp active whole wheat sourdough starter (see resources page)

Mix all ingredients until there are no lumps or dry flour in the bowl. Cover with a clean, damp dish towel or plastic wrap and leave in a draft-free place at room temperature for 12–15 hours. When it is ready, the mix will have expanded to 2–2½ times its original size.

BREAD DOUGH

3 cups whole wheat flour
1¾ cups water, warm to the touch
2 tsp salt
All sourdough mix (recipe above)

MIXING

Place the flour, water, salt and sourdough mix in a large bowl. Mix together just enough to combine the ingredients. Cover with a clean, damp dish towel or plastic wrap to prevent the surface from drying out and let rest for 20 minutes.

KNEADING

Place the dough on a clean work surface, no flour needed. Gently pull the edge of the dough that is closest to your body toward yourself until it won't go any farther without tearing. Fold the dough in half, and then turn it 90 degrees clockwise. Use a dough scraper to loosen the dough if it sticks to your work surface. Continue to stretch, fold and turn the dough for 8–10 minutes. The dough will change over this time, getting stronger and sticking to the work surface less and less. Form the dough into a ball, and place it into a bowl that is lightly dusted with flour. Cover with a clean, damp dish towel or plastic wrap and leave in a draft-free place at room temperature for 45 minutes.

FOLDING

Scrape the dough onto a very lightly floured surface without tearing it. Gently stretch the edges from the center in four directions, as far as you can without tearing it. Starting with the edge closest to you, fold the stretched dough back to the center. Next, do this with the edge opposite you. Then, fold in the left edge, and finally, the one on the right. Dust the bowl with a little more flour and return the dough to the bowl with the smooth side up. Cover it with a clean, damp dish towel or plastic wrap, and let it rest for 45 minutes. Repeat the folding process two more times, resting the dough for 45 minutes between each folding. After the third time, let the dough rest, covered, for one hour.

SHAPING

Lightly coat the inside of your loaf pan (8" x 4") with oil or a nonstick spray. Sprinkle your work surface lightly with flour. Put your dough on the floured surface with the smooth side down, being careful not to tear it. Lightly pat the dough down into a rectangle no wider than your loaf pan. Starting at one end, roll the dough into a log, pinching the end to seal it. Place the dough log in the pan with the pinched side down. Cover the pan with a clean, damp dish towel or plastic wrap and let the dough rise in a draft-free place for three hours.

BAKING

Place your oven rack in the lower third of the oven. Preheat the oven to 450°F for 20–30 minutes before you are ready to bake. Uncover the loaf pan and place it in the oven. Close the oven door and lower the temperature to 425°F. Bake for 40–45 minutes or until the loaf is nicely browned on top. Remove the loaf from the oven, turn it out of the pan, and place on a wire rack to cool.

HAVE FUN!

ABOUT THE BREAD LAB
AT WASHINGTON STATE UNIVERSITY, MOUNT VERNON

The Bread Lab is just what it sounds like: a laboratory where we work together on the science, art and poetry of bread! Here, in Washington State's Skagit Valley, scientists, grain farmers, millers, chefs, bakers, students and educators have gathered since 2008 to research how to make the most flavorful and nutritious food possible, starting with the crops.

We are creating brand-new varieties of wheat that farmers can successfully grow in our fertile region. We then experiment with those varieties to find the best uses for them in baking. Will a specific type of 100% whole wheat flour make a wonderful cookie? A delicious tortilla? Or the perfect loaf of bread?

This is where science factors in to what we do. Can we reproduce the results of our experiments in the fields, in the mills and in the kitchen? Can others do so, too?

For many of the diverse cultures around the globe, our bread defines who we are. Let's all make and enjoy bread together!

—**Dr. Stephen S. Jones**, Director, The Bread Lab

ABOUT THE CREATORS

KIM BINCZEWSKI

Raised on a small farm in New York State, I spent summers in the field pulling weeds, picking up potatoes and—my least favorite task—picking beans. I did not always like the work but I loved being outside… and eating fresh vegetables! When I got older, I went on to study environmental science. I'm sure it was all that hard work that gave me an appreciation for real food, where it comes from, and the value of supporting farms in our communities.

Each day, my work at the Bread Lab is filled with discovery… Not just about science and baking but also about art, literature, music, and the world around us. The best part about working in the lab is the mix of science, farming and baking that makes better food for people and better crops to enrich our soil. I hope you find your own unique mix that brings you joy and makes you curious.

Kim Binczewski is the managing director of the Bread Lab at Washington State University in Mount Vernon, where her work includes field research, community outreach, and connecting farmers with bakers, chefs and businesses. She lives with her family in Bellingham, Washington. Bread Lab! is her first picture book.

BETHANY ECONOPOULY

I have spent my life working with food—a basic necessity for all people. When I was young, I wanted a career baking and cooking. Later, I became fascinated with science and specialized in agriculture. As an agricultural scientist, I depend on repeated experimentation to help keep plants, the environment and people healthy.

Baking sourdough bread is a great way to begin making food yourself. Starting with wheat seeds, microorganisms and water, you can create a delicious loaf of bread. What can you learn about yourself and the world by keeping a starter, measuring ingredients, folding dough, feeling, smelling, tasting and sharing a loaf of sourdough bread? I challenge you to give it a try.

Bethany Econopouly has a PhD from Washington State University and an MS from Colorado State University, both in the agricultural sciences. She previously worked at the Bill & Melinda Gates Foundation in Seattle. She currently lives near Philadelphia. This is her first picture book.

HAYELIN CHOI, ILLUSTRATOR

When I was growing up in Korea, my breakfast was bread baked from the local bakery because my mom rarely had time to prepare a typical Korean breakfast—rice with side dishes. But she would take the time to put strawberry jam on my toasted bread in the morning, and that smell, texture and taste still means so much warmth and love to me.

Hayelin Choi made her picture-book debut illustrating Alice Waters and the Trip to Delicious, which earned a starred review from School Library Journal. She was born and raised in Gwacheon, South Korea, then moved to Toronto and New York City. A visual storyteller, she studied illustration at the School of Visual Arts and is pursuing a graduate degree in graphic design at Maryland Institute College of Art in Baltimore, where she lives.

RESOURCES FOR CURIOUS BAKERS

WEBSITES & VIDEOS

The Bread Bakers Guild of America
Promotes baking education and provides support to professional and home bakers.
www.bbga.org

The Bread Lab at Washington State University, Mount Vernon
www.thebreadlab.wsu.edu

King Arthur Flour
Offers recipes, curriculum ideas and classes—including at the Bread Lab—for both children and adults.
www.kingarthurflour.com

Here are four King Arthur Flour resources that are especially useful for beginners:

Making Your Sourdough Starter
https://www.kingarthurflour.com/recipes/sourdough-starter-recipe

Sourdough Bread: Feeding Your Starter
www.youtube.com/watch?v=_XRqtwN29HU

Sourdough Bread: Making the Dough
www.youtube.com/watch?v=h5aZ9oVTD-o

Sourdough Bread: Shaping and Baking the Bread
www.youtube.com/watch?v=VuIT0RJDdZ8

MORE ABOUT THE BREAD LAB

These in-depth articles, all easy to locate online, further explore the Bread Lab at Washington State University, Mount Vernon.

Binczewski, Kim. "You Can Grow Grains Here." *Vashon-Maury Island Beachcomber*, October 26, 2016

Econopouly, Bethany, and Dr. Stephen Jones. "Redefining Bread." *Huffington Post*, September 23, 2014

Jabr, Ferris. "Bread Is Broken." The *New York Times Magazine*, October 29, 2015

Jones, Stephen S., and Bethany F. Econopouly. "Breeding Away from All Purpose." *Agroecology and Sustainable Food Systems* (Vol. 42, No. 6), January 29, 2018

Ray, Joe. "Wheat Nerds and Scientists Join Forces to Build a Better Bread." *Wired*, August 4, 2017